BLEAK PRECISION

BLEAK PRECISION
A GREG CHAPMAN CHAPBOOK

TABLE OF CONTENTS

ALSO BY GREG CHAPMAN

HOLLOW HOUSE
THE NOCTUARY: PANDEMONIUM
THE FOLLOWERS
TORMENT
THE LAST NIGHT OF OCTOBER
NETHERKIND
THIS SUBLIME DARKNESS AND OTHER DARK STORIES
VAUDEVILLE AND OTHER NIGHTMARES

KAKOPHONY

Please, don't hurt me.
I told you what would happen if you didn't do what I said.
Don't tell mummy what we do, okay?
The fucker's been giving me grief for years. If he comes near me I'm going to fucking smash him.
But they're children in there!
Shut the fuck up you bitch! Shut your fucking mouth or I will split you open!
Every time you touch me, I feel sick. Every time you look at me I want to gouge your eyes out!
Hail Mary, full of Grace, the Lord is with thee…
I just don't want to be here anymore…no one wants me to be here….

Voices.
I hear them all time. When I am awake and when I am asleep. They're always there, in my head, like grains of glass in deep in my brain. I don't know who they are or whether they are real, but each voice is distinct, personal, violent and pleading. Some are victims, but most of them are perpetrators. I hate hearing them the most. I first started hearing voices when I turned sixteen. The first voice was a child, a little boy, a soft voice begging for help. I thought I was going mad, or that someone was playing a joke on me, but every day the voice was there ringing in my ears.

Over time I got used to his voice and I tried to talk to him, but he couldn't hear me. It was only a one way conversation. His pleas for help eventually became cries of pain and I knew that someone somewhere was hurting him. His words receded to muffles and then they stopped altogether. I didn't know why I had to listen to it, but it was clear that somehow I had been tuned into people around me, like I was a living hidden microphone.

It wasn't long after the boy's voice disappeared that more voices came.

They came like a wave, words of fear and anger and murder and rage, each and every one. The crescendo of voices was endless and sometimes they shout over the top of each other. There are so many people out there suffering and I am the only one who can hear them.

It will only hurt for a little while.

I tried to go to the doctor about it, but I am worried that he will commit me or something. I don't want to go to hospital and be locked away. I just need help. I feel so alone because no one knows what I am hearing. I am alone, with the voices.

He's such a fucking wanker, I wish he was dead!

The sound is so real and deafening. All those people suffering and I can't do a damned thing about it. God, I wish it would stop. I can't take it anymore; the crying and the screaming. I just want them to shut up. I can't sleep anymore and my ears are bleeding. There's blood on my pillow and my head is pounding. Please, God help me.

There is no God. God is just a big fucking joke!

I walk around the house at night, shaking in the darkness. I've tried sleeping pills and tranquilsers, but nothing works! They still scream at me. Why is this happening to me? What did I do to deserve this? Someone please tell me what is happening to me.

Look at her, she's fucking wasted!

Let's take her out the back.

The shaking won't stop and the voices are now a million fold. I feel like my head is going to explode.

You fucking bitch! What the fuck do you call this cause it certainly isn't fucking food!

You'll suck it or you'll feel cold steel between your ribs.

The test results have come back…it's a brain tumour.

Oh, please, I don't want to hear it anymore. Stop it. Stop it. Stop it! Stop it! Stop it!

Please God make them go away. Make them leave me alone! Just get out of my head!

God isn't doing this.

What? Who said that? Can you hear me?

The voices have stopped. There is only one voice and its talking to me.

Of course I'm talking to you. Who else would I be talking to?

Oh, God. Who is this? Who are you? How did you make the voices go away?

What voices? I don't hear any voices.

The voices in my head! Can't you hear them? They've been screaming at me for so long!

I told you, I don't hear any voices. I can only hear you.

The voice is indistinct, different from the rest. It's androgynous. I've never heard a voice like it before.

Wait, are you saying that I'm one of the voices in your head?

Yes, you just broke through all the others and they've all gone quiet. I don't know how you did it, but you must have some sort of a gift. You must be special or something.

Special? I've never been special. I always stayed in the background and let the world pass me by. I never talked to anyone. I'm a loner and I like it that way.

Well, I am so glad you're here now. You made the voices go away.

So, you're not hearing any voices now?

Well, except for yours, no.

How do you think you can hear me?

I don't know. One day the voices came into my head, like someone turned on a switch. They've been with me ever since. I've tried to get rid of them for years, but they just keep coming.

Why do you think you can hear them? Have you ever thought about that?

I, I guess I never listened to people, not my mum or dad, no one. I just did my own thing. But I can't understand why I'm hearing such horrible things.

What horrible things?

People hurting each other and people in pain; it's just so awful. But now all I can hear is you.

Sounds like you're crazy.

But how can I be, I'm talking to you.

You're talking to a voice.

But, you're a real person aren't you? You're somewhere out there. Tell me where you are.

I'm not anywhere.

What do you mean?

It's dark. I can't see anything. I can only hear you.

But all those voices are real aren't they? They're real people, I heard them.

But they're just voices. You've never seen anyone. You only hear them. Isn't that what you said?

Yes, but...

I think you need to get help.

But you're talking to me! You can hear what I am saying! We're talking

9

to each other!

You are crazy! Maybe you're hearing voices because you're crazy. Crazy, crazy crazy, crazy!

Shut up! Shut up! Don't say that! I'm not crazy! Just stop talking!

You know how you can get me to stop talking? How to get all of us to stop talking?

Please…

You know what to do. You know what to do. You just go off and do it.

Then he's gone and the voices are coming back in a raging torrent. My head is splitting and I crawl across the floor to the kitchen.

You fucking maniac! I'm gonna fucking kill you.

Oh, God, there's blood.

In all my years, I've never seen anything like this.

What the fuck is wrong with people?

108 people dead. Oh, Christ.

Bless me father, for I have sinned…

I manage to reach the knife block and the large bladed kitchen knife clatters to the floor. Its glimmering edge beckons me and I plunge it deep into my ear.

Silence is golden.

HORROR FICTION: A BLEAK AND DEPRESSING LOOK AT TRUTH

(FIRST PUBLISHED AT INKHEIST.COM, MAY, 2018)

My writing has often been described as "bleak", "depressing", with "unlikeable characters". I take these comments as compliments because after all, aren't I writing horror?

I'm not sure what readers are expecting when they pick up a horror novel. If you read one of mine, I can guarantee that you'll more than likely discover a series of "unlikeable characters" trapped in a "bleak" or "depressing" setting. I'm only holding a mirror up to reality. Sure my stories have a heady dose of the supernatural too, but in the end I'm fascinated by the human condition and just how fucked up people were well before the monsters arrived.

The latest "bleak", "depressing" thing I've had published is *Pandemonium*, the next chapter in my mythos, based upon *The Noctuary*. When I first wrote the original novella way back in 2009 I was trying to answer the question of where my story ideas came from. I took this literally and created a hellish muse who forces a writer to rewrite history. The follow up, *Pandemonium* was me trying to answer the question: where does evil come from? Is it all in our minds? Did we ignite the spark ourselves, or was it put there?

The thing is I'm not really a bleak or unlikeable person. I'm probably a cynic, heavily influenced by my years as a newspaper reporter, covering things like murders, and traffic accidents, scandals and the occasional morning tea fundraiser. Thing is the media is all about bad news; taking the bleak and depressing and ramming it down our throats (I no longer work in the media obviously). It's hard not to be affected by that day in and day out. So yeah, my writing is going to be a reflection of the world as I see it.

My Bram Stoker Award-nominated novel *Hollow House* was about the horrible secrets people hide behind closed doors. My novella *The Eschatologist* was about the "faithful" taking their faith to the extreme after the end of the world. Bleak and depressing, right? Sure, but there's an element of truth as well. Domestic abuse is real and "faith" is sending the world mad – so of course I'm going to use these themes in my stories.

If anything, I'm hoping that after reading my stories, readers will ask themselves the same questions. Seek their own truths. What kind of world are we living in? What kind of person am I? What can I do to try and change these things?

Good horror should always pose these questions and go beyond the blood and gore, or at least use it to paint a picture of humanity. If you're a writer, or aspire to be one, be bleak and depressing, make your characters unlikeable, but most of all tell the truth.

THE PEST CONTROLLER'S WIFE

Selena Berns awoke to the sound of scratching.

The noise was faint, a gentle scraping coming from the walls of the bedroom. It was the same way she awoke every morning, like some sort of alarm clock that worked by sending goose bumps through the flesh. Selena gritted her teeth in frustration and rolled onto her side to alert her husband to the noise, but his side of the bed was cold.

She scanned the room for him, quickly finding his tall frame hunched over an ironing board in the corner. The rising sun cast a sickly yellow glow on his bare chest and back. Steam from the iron hissed loudly as he pressed his uniform.

'Those damned mice are in the walls again,' Selena snapped. 'When are you going to get rid of them, Shaun?'

At first Shaun ignored her, focussed only on removing the creases in his navy blue shirt. The bright yellow embroidered insignia of a cockroach on the chest pocket gleamed.

'I haven't had the chance,' Shaun replied, not looking at her.

Selena stood and pulled her nightgown over her thighs, seemingly self-conscious. 'You could've done it on the weekend.'

Shaun flipped his shirt over and began to press the back. 'I had to do the inventory on the weekend, Selena – you knew that.'

'Well, I'm sick of that noise Shaun – you have to get rid of them. I don't want them in my house. They're disgusting.'

Shaun turned, a stern look on his face, a handsome face, but one that carried very little expression these days. For months Selena had wondered who her husband was and when he had changed.

'I'll get to it eventually,' he told her. 'Okay?'

13

He shook the residual heat out of the shirt and slipped it over his arms, almost ceremoniously. Selena hated Shaun's job; the thought of him chasing rodents and spraying bugs, but it put food on the table and he seemed dedicated to making a living from it.

'Do I have to pay you to get it done?' she said.

'What?'

'Well, you're quite happy to run off to stranger's homes and kill their pests – what about the ones in our house?'

Shaun chuckled and shook his head. 'You're the one who doesn't want the chemicals near the house.'

'That's to protect the kids Shaun,' she replied.

Shaun grimaced and refocussed on buttoning his shirt. He turned his back on Selena and considered himself in the mirror.

'I have to go to work,' he said.

Shaun hardly spoke another word to Selena or the kids at breakfast. In fact, he didn't even eat breakfast. He was engrossed with his job, silently scanning the list on his clipboard of homes he had to visit that day. Homes reportedly infested with pests.

Selena tried not to listen to the scratching in the walls as she spoon-fed their six-month-old daughter Karen. Her young ears were not mature enough to hear the crawling din. She made her own noise by slapping her hands on the high chair.

Their older daughter Anne however was well aware of the scratching.

'Do we have mice?' she asked.

Shaun turned to look at Anne warily.

'Yes, we do, honey,' her mother said, glaring at her husband from across the breakfast table. 'Daddy's going to get rid of them soon.'

Shaun's eyes shifted to his wife. 'I told you I would get rid of them when I had the chance! He slammed the clipboard on the table, rattling his untouched plate of eggs on toast. The scratching suddenly ceased.

'Don't you yell at me, Shaun,' Selena said. 'All I'm asking is for you to throw a bait in there or something. Anything!'

Shaun gathered his clipboard and mobile telephone and put on his coat. Selena could see his face burning with suppressed rage. What on earth is wrong with him, she wondered. Before she could raise her concern he was headed for the front door, bag in hand. He hadn't even packed a lunch.

'Shaun – wait,' Selena called.

The door slammed and the scratching started all over again.

One hundred and ninety-three Harrington Street was the first job on Shaun's list.

PEST~ICIDE was one of the largest pest control and extermination companies in the country, with more than fifty stations across Australia. Its exterminators had the ability and the capacity to find, capture and exterminate all pests of the vermin or insect variety.

Shaun became an exterminator when he was twenty-five, three years before he met Selena. Six months later she became pregnant with Anne. Seven years on and they'd added Karen to the fold. Shaun was happy and he loved his kids, but since Karen's birth Selena had become difficult and critical of Shaun's line of work.

Being a pest controller meant the world to Shaun. It was his lifeblood and with Selena a stay-at-home mum, his job was the family's only source of income. Yet it was more than a job, Shaun knew he was providing a service. He was taking away insects and vermin that people didn't want around them. He was separating species that didn't deserve to live together in the same home.

He parked his bright yellow PEST~ICIDE work van in the driveway of number one ninety-three Harrington and re-checked the work sheet. "Possible cockroach infestation" was written in the complaint column. Cockroaches were all too common in unkempt homes, but number one ninety-three looked like it belonged to a well-to-do family or couple.

A tall blonde woman, about thirty-five answered the door. She looked quite stunning with her tight tan slacks, cashmere sweater and pearl earrings.

'Oh, you're finally here,' she said. 'Thank goodness. These bugs are all over the place and I don't know why.'

'Mrs Campion is it?' Shaun inquired.

'Yes, that's right.'

'My name's Shaun and I'm a pest controller from PEST~ICIDE.'

'Please come in – and call me Judy.'

Shaun stepped into a wide vestibule decorated with marble floors and an oak spiral staircase. A bust of some unknown bald man sat on the mantelpiece. Shaun was right; the cockroaches certainly didn't belong in such a place.

'Could you please show me where the cockroaches are?'

'Of course, this way,' Judy said, smiling pleasantly as she led Shaun through the lavish living room with its ornate coffee table and fireplace to the kitchen.

'They started coming out from under the sink the other morning,' Judy explained. 'It was just awful! One of them crawled up my leg.'

Shaun crouched and opened the doors of the sink cupboard. At least one cockroach retreated from the daylight into a small hole in the corner.

'Oh, I see,' Shaun said. 'Yep, just as I thought.'

'Is it bad?' Judy said, chewing her fingernails.

'The cockroaches have eaten a hole in your cupboard and they're coming into the house that way. You see these little brown flecks? That's cockroach faeces and quite a lot of it. And those little white things there? They're eggs. I'd say you've definitely got an infestation here.'

He turned to her, smiling. 'Did you know that out of the four thousand species of cockroach in the world, only thirty species cohabitate with humans and only four species are considered pests.'

Judy swallowed. 'Um, no I didn't know that – can you kill them? I've got a dinner party this weekend and I'd hate for one of the guests to see those horrible things in my house.'

Shaun set bag on the breakfast bar and added considerably more professionalism to his smile. 'Of course I'll remove them for you.'

The rest of Shaun's workday was quite busy. After he finished at the Campion home he had to deal with a rat up a drainpipe at an old people's home (the metaphor didn't get past the residents) and a minor red back spider infestation at a doctor's surgery in the city.

After clocking off at the office and filling in the appropriate paperwork, Shaun set off for home, dreading his wife's persistent demands. At least insects and vermin didn't make demands.

The scratching in the walls was slowly driving Selena insane.

The mice seemed to be concealed in the hallway, the kitchen and even the bathroom. She could imagine them leaving their filth in the wall space, their little incisors tearing through plasterboard. The thought of their hairy little shapes scurrying about while she slept made her want to retch.

She would demand Shaun get rid of them when he got home.

No, she didn't need him to get rid of the pests – she could do it herself. She told Anne to put on her shoes and bundled her and Karen in the car. They drove eight blocks to the corner store.

'What are we buying Mummy?' Anne asked.

Selena grabbed six mousetraps off the shelf and smiled widely. The mice would never know what hit them.

And Shaun?

He'd get the surprise of his life when he saw he wasn't the man of the house anymore.

Selena was dusting off her hands when Shaun arrived home.

From the moment he closed the door he refused to look at her, but he enthusiastically hugged and kissed the children. She knew he found her annoying, a nagger, but she didn't care. He needed to take responsibility for his life outside of work. Perhaps her actions that afternoon would set him right?

'I went out and got some mousetraps,' she told Shaun.

Shaun stopped dead and almost dropped Karen to the floor. His face drained of blood.

'You what?'

'I couldn't wait for you to get rid of them anymore so I went down and bought some. I just finished setting them.'

Shaun sprinted out of the living room down the hallway. He was in a mad panic. Selena's heart pounded and her mind burned.

'Where did you put them?' Shaun cried.

'What? Why – what in God's name is wrong with you Shaun?'

Shaun whirled on her, his face sweaty, eyes afire.

'WHERE DID YOU PUT THE TRAPS BITCH!'

Selena went to the girls, desperate to protect them. Shaun was enraged, searching cupboards and bedrooms. The girls began to cry as their father bellowed and wailed.

'Please Shaun – they're just mice!' Selena begged.

Shaun was about to scream when a sharp crack struck the air – the sound of a mousetrap serving its purpose. Tears began to well up in his eyes.

'NO!'

He turned and followed the noise, hurling himself down the kitchen steps to the laundry. Selena was afraid to follow, but her mind craved reason; she needed to know why her husband was overwrought with grief over the death of something he'd spent years exterminating.

'Shaun!'

Then she found him, cradling the mousetrap in his hands, its prey dangling lifeless, its spine broken in two. Shaun was crying and tracing the mouse's fur with trembling fingers. After a moment, he lifted the steel mechanism and freed the mouse's body. The sight sickened Selena.

'What are you doing?'

Shaun considered her with dark eyes before he gently placed the mouse on the ground. He strode to her and grabbed her by the hair.

'Where are the rest?'

'I ...'

'WHERE!'

'Over there!' Selena pointed to a space behind the washing machine.

'No!' Shaun raced to the spot and wrenched the washing machine out of the way. Selena's stomach lurched when she saw what was behind it; a hole, about a foot wide, infested with tiny mice, dozens and dozens of them. She expected them to flee, but they seemed to huddle around Shaun, circling his shoes, almost with affection. To her horror she watched Shaun kick away the mousetrap.

'Oh, God Shaun! What's happened to you!'

Shaun urged the mice back into the hole with tender touches and the vermin complied. He replaced the washing machine and approached his terror-stricken wife.

'Do you really want to know?' he sneered.

He grabbed her by the hair again and dragged her up the stairs. Karen and Anne shrieked with fear, as their mother's own screams resounded inside the house. The children watched helplessly as their father threw her before the refrigerator. As Shaun pulled on the fridge and freed it from its cavity in the kitchen, a drawing of Shaun with "I love Daddy" in Anne's crude writing, fluttered through the air to the floor.

Hundreds of cockroaches burst out from the wall behind the fridge, flying and crawling across every surface, spreading and spreading, closer and closer to Selena and her children. Shaun smiled at them, like a proud father would his children.

'This is my family,' he told Selena. 'My children.'

Selena screamed as the cockroaches followed Shaun into the living room. The pest controller sat in his chair and the insects swarmed all over him, on his arms and hair and face until all you could see were his eyes, dark and staring.

'I saved them all,' he said with squirming lips. One cockroach seemed to kiss him. 'I've always saved them. They deserve to live too, even more so than you.'

He gazed at his wife as she cradled herself and her children in the corner of the room – like creatures that feared something greater than them.

As the mice joined the ever shifting, twitching throng that covered their master, Shaun reached into his bag and retrieved a large box of Ratsak. Then his voice rose above the scratching:

'I think you need an exterminator.'

FASCINATION

It started out as a curiosity.

Julie and Paul shared a common interest and therefore an unwavering attraction to each other.

She was the only daughter of a surgeon; he was the son of a baker. They were an unlikely combination, but there was much more than a physical and personal connection between them.

What they shared was secret and unspoken.

I'll never forget when Julie first met Paul in the hospital where here father worked.

The nurses, who always seemed to study Julie with vindictive eyes, pointed her in the direction of the morgue when she asked for her father.

The morgue was an enticing place, cold and curiously bland – like a blank canvas. The steel doors, which sealed off the modern-day tombs, gleamed in the fluorescent light. A sharp, sickly sweet scent of chemicals lingered in the air and you couldn't help but feel invigorated.

Julie found her father standing next to a corpse, lying on an autopsy table – a long, fresh, red Y-shaped scar dominating the body. The doctor was scanning an open medical file when he looked up and saw his daughter.

'Julie. For god's sake what are you doing down here?' he said.

Julie couldn't take her eyes off the body; his slightly parted mouth, the half-closed eyes, the small line of dried blood on his left arm.

'They told me you were down here,' she replied.

'What do you want? Can't you see that I'm busy?'

Julie wanted to reach out and touch the dead man, to feel his death.

'What happened to him?' she muttered.

Her father stared down at the dead man. There was so much guilt in the doctor's eyes.

'He died,' he told her.

'How?'

Frustration suddenly burned in her father's eyes. 'That's what I'm trying to find out Julie,' he snapped. 'Now if you could please just tell me what you want?'

Julie tore her gaze away from the body.

'I need … some money.'

'What for?'

Julie shrugged and looked at a series of X-rays on the far wall; images of cracked skulls and shattered pelvis's shone back at her, blue on black.

'I … to go to the movies … with Cindy,' she said.

Julie wondered whether the look her father was giving her was the same one he gave to his medical students when they messed up. She watched as he took out his wallet and crumpled a fifty-dollar note into her hand.

'Fine,' he told her. 'Just don't be out late. I should be home about ten.'

'Thanks,' Julie replied with a morose tone. She took one last look at the dead man before heading for the door. There was such compassion in her eyes.

The double doors of the morgue slid closed behind Julie, making a sucking sound that reverberated around the hall. She watched her father through the viewing window. He tossed the file to the floor and grabbed a post-mortem tool off a nearby tray and started to pull the staples out of the dead man's chest, one-by-one. You could almost feel them being wrenched free.

Julie was startled to find a young man standing beside her.

He was tall and thin; with scruffy brown hair and blue eyes that shone brightly against the teal medical scrubs he was wearing. There was such life in his eyes.

'He had a heart attack on the operating table,' he told her.

'Sorry?' Julie said.

'He died on the table about a week ago.' He pointed to Julie's father. 'That guy did the operation.'

'That's my Dad,' Julie said.

'Oh, sorry.'

'That's okay.' Julie pushed her auburn hair behind an ear and smiled nervously. 'Do you work here – in the morgue?'

'Yeah, I keep the place clean. My name's Paul.'

Julie shook his hand. 'Julie.'

They both turned to watch Julie's father, who had re-opened the dead man's chest. The ragged, bloody viscera enthralled Julie.

'You probably shouldn't look at this,' Paul said.

'No … it's okay. It's interesting.'

Paul sniggered. 'Do you want to be a surgeon or something?'

Julie watched her father remove a sizeable portion of the dead man's

21

ribcage.

'No, it's not that. I just find it … fascinating.'

'Dead people?'

Julie nodded. 'Isn't that why you work here?'

'Yeah, I guess it's pretty cool. I get to see some weird stuff.'

Julie's eyes beamed. 'What kind of stuff?'

*

Julie and Paul waited another two hours for her father to leave. They stood in the car park and after they watched him drive away with a flustered look on his face, they ventured back inside.

Julie's heart pounded with excitement; the prospect of being caught was almost too much to bear. Paul was obviously getting a kick out of it too and Julie sensed that he had taken a liking to her. You could see it in their eyes. She had to admit that she thought he was cute, but she was more attracted to what he did for a living.

The elevator stopped at the morgue. Butterflies swirled in Julie's stomach and she felt an almost overwhelming sense of reverence when they stepped into the autopsy room.

Julie read all the names on each steel door of the mortuary refrigerator – the names of the dead. She thought about the dead man.

'Where is the man who my father operated on?' she asked Paul.

Paul took her hand. 'I've got something much better.'

They left the autopsy room, through a service door and walked down a flight of internal stairs. The sounds of huge air-conditioning fans and steam pipes whirred around in the air. Julie had no idea where Paul was going, but she wasn't scared. She trusted him. Paul opened another door and a wave of heat hit Julie in the face. She saw half a dozen large waste disposal bins surrounding a massive furnace. Paul opened one of the bins.

'It's medical waste,' he said. 'Organs, limbs, you name it.'

Julie took a look in the bin and her insides trembled. 'Yuck!'

'How can this gross you out, but you have no problems watching a dead man getting cut up?'

'I don't know. He was dead, but all these … bits…. belonged to live people.'

Paul shrugged. 'Yeah, well, they're still pretty cool.' He suddenly leaned into her ear. 'You know what? I took one of them home.'

Julie backed away, shocked. 'You stole one?'

'It was just a hand, that's all. It was cut off some guy who died … I think he had gangrene or something.'

'What did you do with it?'

Paul smiled. 'I preserved it. I've got it in a jar in my bedroom. I can bring it in if you'd like?'

Julie imagined the hand slowly pickling in the jar. Death suspended in solution.

'Okay,' she said, smiling. 'I'll meet you back here tomorrow night.'

*

Julie kept smiling on the train home. Paul's good looks and his exciting promises of secrets and wonders had re-energised her. He knew a lot about the process of dying and Julie knew he would show her whatever she wanted.

Her mother wouldn't approve of him, she thought to herself. But then, her mother was dead. She died a long time ago, when Julie was just three years old. Her mother had been driving home from work when a drunk, driving on the freeway, crossed onto the other side of the road and hit her mother's SUV – head on.

In the years since, Julie managed to find out little pieces of information about the crash. The car the drunk was driving was doing 110kmh when it slammed into her mother's vehicle. The force of the impact put the engine of the SUV in her lap and her face was torn to shreds by metal and glass fragments. They had to use dental records to identify her.

Julie's father was devastated, but Julie was too young to really understand. She cried for her mother, but it wasn't until her pre-teens that the fact her mother would never be around finally sunk in. Her father refocussed on his job and Julie knew deep down that every patient death brought back his grief.

As the world beyond the train blurred by, Julie realised it was probably her investigations into the tragedy that first piqued her morbid interests. She supposed that in order to grieve, she needed to understand what happened and how it happened.

Julie craved the images on the nightly news; the war on terror, the starving children, the car pile-ups on the freeway. Those stories were the best; they put her at the scene of her mother's own demise.

But now Paul would give her all the access she needed; death as fresh as it could be.

Julie got off at her station and walked about six blocks to her home. She enjoyed walking at night. The darkness seemed to embrace her and the world looked so different and comforting.

Her father was waiting for her at the front door, looking livid.

'Where the hell have you been? I almost called the police.'

'I went to the movies,' Julie said as she went inside.

'Don't give me that! I rang Cindy and she said she hadn't seen you. Where were you?'

What a bitch that Cindy was, Julie thought. She could have just lied.

'I didn't want to go to the movies … so I just went for a walk.'

'For a walk - do you know how dangerous that is?

Julie pushed past her father and walked upstairs, to her bedroom. 'I was fine Dad. Nothing is going to happen to me.'

'That's easy for you to say! You're not the one sitting here worrying that you might be lying in a ditch or dead!'

Julie slammed her door and climbed into bed. She wasn't interested in eating or speaking to her father. But as her eyelids got heavier she couldn't help but agree with his idea that she could be dead somewhere.

*

Julie stayed in her room the next day. Her father as usual, left for work, assuming that she would eventually rise and go to school. How wrong he was; how wrong he was about everything to do with her.

Some time after 10 a.m. Julie went to shower and found herself captivated by her naked form in the mirror. Her skin was so pale and her deep auburn hair beamed like fresh blood. She imagined her clean skin black and bruised with putrefaction. She wondered what it would feel like to be the dead man in the morgue, all cold and calm.

Later, she ran a razor blade up the inside of her thigh and just watched the blood crawl down to her toes. She stared as the blood congealed and imagined the cells withering and dying. She did the same to her other leg.

She looked in the mirror again, but this time the dead man from the morgue was standing in her place looking back at her – there was so much sadness in her eyes. But with a blink, she realised he was gone.

About 2 p.m. she raided her father's liquor cabinet and numbed the pain with three fingers of bourbon. She savoured the tingling sensation in her arms. Then she fell asleep.

*

Julie was woken by the sound of her father coming home and she scrambled to lock up his cabinet and sneak out the back door. It was dusk as she walked to the train station and Paul entered her thoughts for the first time in twelve hours. She couldn't wait to see him and to smell his world again.

About half an hour later she met him at the back entrance to the hospital, just as they agreed. She saw his smile and watched his eyes undress her. His skin was pale too and she found herself imagining what their bodies would look like together.

Paul took her inside the ice-cold morgue and produced the jar with the hand inside. The gangrenous appendage lolled about in the brine-coloured liquid.

'What do you think?' Paul said.

'It's …' Julie couldn't respond. The hand looked fake when it was disconnected from the body. '…okay I guess.'

Paul frowned. 'You don't like it do you?'

'It's not that,' Julie replied, suddenly reaching for him. 'It's just not the same.'

'As the dead guy … I know.'

He looked away, thoughts tumbling around in his mind. Then, he moved to the steel doors where the bodies laid and opened one. He slid out a drawer to reveal the dead man's corpse. Julie's heart leapt.

She went to the body and just stared at it.

'There's no one here,' Paul said. 'We've got the whole place to ourselves.'

Julie smiled and took the dead man's hand in hers. You could almost feel her the hotness of her blood. She smiled even wider.

Warmth radiated through Paul as he watched her. The way that she looked at the dead man was just too much. He walked around behind her and held her, his fingers gliding over her clothes and feeling the ample roundness of her breasts. Paul felt her lean into him and she tilted her head back to plunge her tongue into his mouth.

They caressed and kissed, savouring the response of their bodies and the immediacy of it. Paul opened one of the steel doors and slid out an empty drawer. He lifted Julie onto it and she moaned as its coldness spread over her back.

Paul pulled off her clothes and ravaged her. He saw the fresh scars on her legs and he couldn't help but kiss them. Minutes later he was inside her and she was thrusting wildly beneath him. Yet she would only look at the dead man. But this only urged him to ravish her again.

When it was done, they laid in each other's arms and felt their hearts trembling. Julie held Paul tight and stared at the dead man. Again her eyes were full of sadness.

Eventually they both began to dress. It was hard for Julie not to stare at the dead man, to let him go. Paul suddenly pushed the drawer closed and locked the door.

'Are you okay?' he asked.

'Yeah…'

Paul went to kiss her, but Julie pulled away.

'What's wrong?' Paul said.

'Nothing.'

Paul grimaced. 'Did I hurt you?'

'No. I liked it. I just …'

'You want to see him again?'

Julie nodded.

'Well, you can't,' Paul replied. 'We have to go. We'll get caught if we stay here.'

Julie felt tears on her cheeks. 'What's going to happen to him?'

Paul took her hand. 'His family will claim him and he'll be buried or cremated or whatever.'

'I'm not going to see him again am I?'

Paul held her close and savoured her love for the dead man.

'I'm sorry.'

*

Paul felt helpless. He was desperate to help Julie, to love her, but he felt like she wouldn't let him in. As he sat alone in the shadows of the morgue, he revisited their lovemaking in his mind. Despite the tenderness they shared, they were still disconnected.

Julie's love for him was strong, but Paul knew she loved the dead man more.

Paul walked to the door that hid the dead man from the world of the living and opened it and pulled out the drawer. The overhead fluorescent lights cast a harsh light on the dead man's blank eyes.

Paul's gaze was just as empty.

*

They met at the train station the next night. The city was wet and murky and the street lamps' mustard coloured light gave everything a lurid texture. Julie loved it. Paul seemed jittery to her, almost to the point of excitement.

'What's going on?' she asked.

'It's a surprise.'

He held her hand and took her over the footbridge, down to the other side of the freeway. The road ran right beside acres of dense parklands. You could almost drink in the solitude. The sounds of the traffic faded as they walked hand-in-hand between the spindly trees.

They'd walked about five hundred metres when Julie saw something lying on the ground. It was a body, wrapped in white plastic. Paul ran to it and pulled the plastic apart to reveal the face of the dead man. He turned to her, smiling.

'Surprise!'

Julie was horrified. 'What have you done?'

'What?'

'You brought him out here? Alone? He was safe at the morgue.'

'What are you talking about? I thought you wanted to see him again?'

'Not like this! You have to take him back!'

Paul was confused; he thought Julie would love him more for the gesture. The body was his gift to her and now she was throwing it back in his face. He reached for her, but she just pulled away.

'Take him back,' she begged him.

'We could keep him,' Paul implored. 'I can put him somewhere nice and cold. We can have him forever.'

Julie was sobbing and as she watched the dead man's body slowly surrendering to the elements, she caught sight of another shape standing nearby.

For the first time, she saw my true form.

I stood over my body, silently screaming at her to let me go. Julie screamed in turn and ran.

Branches swiped at her face as she ran for the bridge, away from me and away from Paul. She could hear Paul calling, but she would never go to him again. He had betrayed her; he had done the unthinkable. She felt that Paul had defiled me.

Rubber screeched beside Julie and she turned to find light piercing her vision. A dull roar shook the air and pain suddenly racked her bones.

The world spun and then there was darkness.

*

Paul screamed at Julie to stop, but it was too late. She never saw the car coming.

The SUV slammed into her and sent her body flying metres into the air. She twisted upside down and fell, her skull coming into direct contact with the road. Blood began to pool around her face seconds later.

Paul didn't know why she ran. He had begged and called to her, but it was as if she didn't want to hear him anymore. He had chased her away – to her death.

Choking back tears, Paul turned away from the sight and ran into the woods, to the place where his world came apart. My dead eyes stared back at him; a stare that his one true love now shared. He never wanted to see her like that, ever.

He wanted to remember her smiling. The way she smiled when we were all together in love. But now she was gone and he couldn't love me without her.

He felt the handle of the knife in his hand, then the tingly touch of the steel. The steel stung his arm as it sliced through the pale blue veins in his wrist. Was this what it felt like when Julie did it?

Soon Paul's blood was soaking the dead leaves at his feet.

As his blood flowed Paul laid down next to my body; the one fascination that had brought he and Julie together. Paul finally revealed his love for me and as the darkness swarmed around him, I held out my hand to him, smiling all the while.

SCAR TISSUE

It never ceased to amaze Jeffrey just how many amputees there were in the city.

Jeffrey only needed to visit any of the seedy bars to find some veteran, or out of work disabled drunk patronising the bar like a bad smell.

It made his task so much easier.

Still, Jeffrey had to be careful; if he was ever caught playing his game it would mean the end of him.

Copperhead Road blared from the jukebox in the corner of the bar, a few drunks already trying to best Cougar-Mellencamp's vocals and failing. The only upside to their frivolity was that it distracted everyone from noticing Jeffrey, or his attire; the heavy coat, gloves, dark jeans and hoodie weren't just to keep out the cold.

Jeffrey sat next to the amputee at the bar and waited for the right moment to start a conversation. His next victim stared into his glass of whiskey as if it was going to tell him his future. The guy was a transhumeral amputee, the left sleeve of his khaki jacket pinned in a neat pouch just above where his elbow should have been. His unshaven face was a mash-up of guilt and pain; no amount of pretence was ever going to hide that. Jeffrey knew that from experience.

'Hey man, what you drinking?' Jeffrey said.

The guy squinted at him. 'Say what?'

'I just want to buy you a drink?' Jeffrey said, trying to look innocent from under the hoodie.

The guy leaned back, his face becoming a cringe. 'What the fuck - you gay or something?'

Jeffrey turned on his seat and showed the man his own transhumeral amputation – but of the right arm.

'Hey, just trying to talk to a fellow brother in arms,' Jeffrey said with the most reassuring smile he could muster.

Jeffrey watched the guy's expression soften, but it was still teetering on the edge of wariness.

'Did you tour?' the barfly asked, and looked Jeffrey up and down.

Jeffrey shook his head and the lurid bar lighting struggled to illuminate his features, He signalled to the barman.

'Give my buddy here another of whatever he's having. I'll have a Johnny Walker, straight up. Jefrrey laid a twenty on the counter and instantly softened his new friend's demeanour.

'The name's Colby,' he said and offered Jeffrey his right hand.

Jeffrey shook Colby's hand with his left. It would have seemed awkward to people who still had the use of all their limbs, but to the fellow amputees, it was like a sacred gang sign. They shared a chuckle and Jeffrey was grateful to see the tension was gone.

'Good to meet you Colby – the name's Jeffrey.'

Colby smiled and Jeffrey noticed a few of his teeth were missing, probably from chugging back so many whiskey's on the government's dime. Yet it wasn't Colby's teeth that Jeffrey needed.

'So, how'd you lose yours? Mine was in Afghanistan. I picked up a rock to toss it at some Afghani kids who were following my unit around. Little did I know there was an IED underneath.'

'Oh, shit, that's messed up,' Jeffrey said with a wince.

'Yeah, well, I was always one to act first and think later.'

The barman returned with their drinks. Jeffrey saw Colby swallow back the remains of his first drink before taking a mouthful of the new one.

'Well, my story isn't as action-packed, sadly,' Jeffrey said.

Colby frowned. Oh, yeah? Don't tell me it was a work accident?'

'Ever heard of necrosis?'

Colby shook his head and took another swig. Jeffrey held out his right arm and rolled back the sleeve to reveal a scarred, wrinkled stump, peppered with pock marks.

'It started out as just a sore, a scab really,' Jeffrey said. Then my whole arm just turned black. Next thing I know I was being rushed to the ER. They almost had to put me on life-support. The surgeon took my arm to save my life. Not much of a life though, right?'

'Jesus,' Colby said, before finishing off his drink. 'Sounds like you're lucky to have survived.

Jeffrey swallowed back his whisky and called the barman over again.

'I'm still surviving – everyday,' he said. 'But not just because I lost my arm. I lost my humanity too. I'm alone.'

Colby nodded. 'I hear you brother.'

*

Jeffrey led a very drunk Colby out the back door of the bar and into a rain-slick alley. No one saw him push the veteran to the ground, but he had to act fast because the alley wouldn't stay empty for long.

His newfound friend moaned and squirmed and Jeffrey had to pin him down with his knees. Jeffrey feared the cold misty rain was going to wash away Colby's inebriation, wash away any chance Jeffrey had. Jeffrey glanced over his shoulder to check for passers-by, and when he was sure the coast was clear, he reached into his jacket.

Colby stirred beneath him and tried to sit up. Jeffrey shoved him back down.

'Stay still,' he hissed.

'What the… fuck?' Colby said and again he tried to sit up.

'Don't move – it will all be over soon.'

'You are a faggot!'

'Shut up!'

Jeffrey pulled the long bladed knife free and plunged it into Colby's right arm. The veteran cried out, but Jeffrey quickly lifted his right knee and pressed it against Colby's throat to silence him. Quickly Jeffrey drew the blade back and forth, slicing through flesh muscle and tendons. Blood spread out onto the asphalt. Just before Colby succumbed to the pain, Jeffrey leaned in to whisper into his ear.

'Don't you remember, Colby? You said you'd give your right arm to be free of the guilt and shame.'

The limb came free with a wet pop. Jeffrey put the knife back in his coat, picked up Colby's severed right arm and held it to his left. The scarred stump of Jeffrey's arm opened like a hungry babe's mouth to receive the new appendage. Within seconds Jeffrey felt a wave of warmth cross the new flesh and when Colby's fingers starting moving to his command, he smiled in satisfaction.

*

Jeffrey awoke in his dank apartment to the hum of phantom limb pain. His new right arm felt cold to the touch, like the rest of him. It was his body's way of accepting the new appendage; with time the numbness would fade and the arm would be part of him, not something he'd simply appropriated.

He studied himself in the bathroom mirror. The new right arm was grey with pallor, while the left hand he'd acquired the month before had only just attained the same hue as the rest of his skin. Thin pale lines around the circumference of his lower legs and around his pelvis were signatures of previous acquisitions. He remembered all of his 'donors', but he felt no sympathy or guilt because his actions had been what the necrosis demanded.

He didn't know why or how the necrosis chose not to kill him all those years ago, all he understood was that it chose to use him. It lie dormant in his cells until, once a month, it became hungry. Every four weeks a finger, or a foot, or even an ear would turn black and the necrosis would demand its share. By feeding it with new pieces of flesh, Jeffrey kept himself alive, but it meant he was nothing more than a serial killer, condemned to a solitary life hiding and murdering. The cycle was starting to wear him down.

Jeffrey showered then dressed in his uniform of anonymity and ventured out into the city. He soaked up the sights and smells of the streets; people going about their daily routines, unaware of the hunter in their midst. He smiled to himself as he rode the subway, the thrill of predation sending goose pimples through his entire body (all except his new right arm, which was still numb). When he was happy the necrosis was happy, but Jeffrey knew that it wouldn't last forever. It wouldn't be long until the cycle turned back towards rotting limbs and hunger. It was as inevitable as the rising of the sun. As the train came to a stop along the city route, Jeffrey noticed a young couple in the back of the carriage. He felt a twinge of as he watched them touching and kissing, as painful as the rot when it came to visit him. Angry, he exited the train, the necrosis' demand to be patient and ignore unnecessary desires trying to console him.

But it wasn't enough anymore.

He wandered the street for the rest of the day, frustration riding his coat tails. The sight of an undressed female mannequin in a shop window stopped him in his tracks. He stood on the sidewalk peering through the glass at the articulated limbs and blank face and realised that the necrosis hadn't given him life at all. In fact it had robbed him of it, and left him to walk the earth as the undead, cursed not just with hunger, but thought.

He wanted his life back and he would take it, or die trying.

*

Jeffrey bided his time. He locked himself away in his apartment until the hunger came. The itch started in his jaw this time and, over several hours, as he paced his bedroom, watching a clear sky turn the colour of gunmetal, the itch intensified into a burn. The burst vein beneath his chin blossomed and blackened, spreading across the map of his face.

It had been several years since the necrosis had chosen his face and it made him wonder whether the disease knew what he had planned. Eventually the pain became so debilitating that it was all Jeffrey could think about. The necrosis' voice pulsed with each wave of pain. Feed, it said, as it opened a hole in his cheek. Feed, as the hole exposed the bone of his upper jaw.

Feed.

And like a good servant, he ventured into the night.

*

Even though the necrosis could get inside Jeffrey's head and order him to kill, he didn't believe it could read his thoughts. This made his plans all the more possible.

Jeffrey walked to the train station, scanned his pass at the gate, careful to cover the festering wound on his face for prying eyes. He went to the first platform and boarded the first train. He resolved to the necrosis' bidding and kill at the first opportunity, but the disease had no say over who he could kill.

Jeffrey rode the train for an hour before a couple got on board. He felt the wave of rage broil inside him as they interlocked their fingers and kissed, but it was the male who angered him the most. From the other end of the carriage, he sized the guy up; he was roughly the same height as Jeffrey, but thicker set, but that didn't matter in the end. All Jeffrey had to do was get him alone.

The couple departed at Gracewell station and Jeffrey exited with them. Keeping his distance was a struggle as they waked hand in hand. He grit his teeth, but it only exacerbated the necrosis, which had now spread to his gums. He drudged along behind the lovers for four blocks before they finally reached their destination – the Temptation Nightclub.

Jeffrey slinked into the line of revellers and paid his dues. The bouncers never paid him any mind. He'd honed his ability to blend in over many years, but he knew that the hastening rot in his face would be impossible to ignore.

He found the furthest booth with a view of the dance floor, beyond the beams of strobing light and watched his couple. There were dozens of partygoers on the dance floor, but they were the only ones he wanted. He was the one, because she was.

The pair danced and fondled, kissed and loved, while he rotted on the sidelines, at the mercy of his monstrousness.

It was time to change the game.

*

Jeffrey waited for the guy to visit the toilet before taking his chance.

The guy was fit to burst, almost knocking over another patron to get

33

to the urinal. Jeffrey slinked into the stall opposite, locked the door and waited.

Jeffrey could imagine what the guy was thinking about; thoughts Jeffrey had never had – until now. Jeffrey was going to be the one to take Claire as his own, not this… waste. As the guy finished pissing and zipped up, Jeffrey flushed and stepped out to face his next victim. They almost collided.

'Hey sorry bro,' the guy said. Then Jeffrey saw the recognition in his eyes. 'Jesus, what is wrong with your face?'

'What's wrong with yours?' Jeffrey replied and he felt his lower jaw wobble.

The guy, his own face contorted with disgust, tried to shift past Jeffrey, but he blocked his path.

'Get the fuck out of my way you freak.'

Jeffrey grabbed the guy's arm, but he wrenched it away and shoved Jeffrey back. He fell back into the stall, rage building in his chest. He wanted to tear the guy's head off right then and there, but when two other men entered the bathroom, the guy fled. Breathing heavy, Jeffrey left the gents and bee-lined through the alcohol-fuelled crowd towards the front door. If the guy was going to leave or report him to security, he had to get outside first.

*

Jeffrey's couple left fifteen minutes later. He saw them emerge into street and stalked them all the way back to the train station. The darkness was his friend, keeping him from sight, but he could see them just fine. Jeffrey's encounter in the bathroom had obviously put the guy off by the way he'd cut their night short and this pleased him greatly.

As barbs of impatient pain spread through his face and neck, Jeffrey got on the train with them, but three carriages back. He stood near the exit, keeping his eyes on the platform at every stop for the couple to appear. The pain reached its peak and stayed there, a feeling of molten glass burrowing into the bone. The necrosis was relentless in its demands for new flesh, leaving Jeffrey shaking and sweating.

The train came to a stop at Rockingham station and to his relief when Jeffrey put a foot out onto the platform, he glimpsed his couple exiting. Jeffrey got off the train just before the doors closed. He slipped between the pools of overhead light and eyed the pair walking up the stairs to street level. Once they reached the top Jeffrey followed their scent - all the way home.

*

Jeffrey's phantom limb pain burned anew as he studied them through the bedroom window of their apartment, watched their hands slide over each's bodies.

He knew what had been missing from his life; he'd not only lost pieces of flesh, but pieces of his soul. The necrosis was the only guardian he'd ever known and it had left him a monster. As the couple stripped off each other's clothing he was reminded how imperfect he was; these lovers carried no scars, only devotion. Jeffrey's devotion to the necrosis had not just left him empty, but left a long line of corpses, mangled and mutilated, in his wake. There would be no more scrounging for scraps, no more amputees or ingrates, no.

The girl withdrew and whispered something in her lover's ear before leaving the room. This was Jeffrey's chance to have what everyone else had. He gripped the downpipe and ascended the wall in the direction of the window. The necrosis scraped at his psyche, always demanding. There was no more time to wait.

Jeffrey pushed the window open. The guy turned aghast, his naked body white with shock at the sight of the intruder. Jeffrey launched himself at the man and brought him to the ground. With old left hand, Jeffrey clamped the man's mouth to stifle any scream. With the knife in his new hand, he slashed open the man's throat, down and through the bone. Blood sprayed out across the floor as Jeffrey wrenched the head free. Quickly he pushed the body under the bed and turned the knife to his own throat.

Jeffrey never felt the sting of the blade, the flesh of his entire head was so necrotic, like a mummified skull coated with tar. Yet he kept working, sawing through the blackened muscles and veins and bone. His head came away from his body much easier than his victim's. He tossed his head aside and with the necrosis guiding him, he picked up it its replacement and attached it with a twist. Within moments, his sight, through new eyes, revealed the room. Quickly, his new head tightening the edges of the neck wound close, he reached for a blanket to wipe away the excess blood, until footsteps echoed from the hall.

He crossed the room to meet her and beheld her naked form. Even in the half-light of the early morning, she was perfect. The touch of her skin made his tingle. She smiled at him and then kissed him deeply. When her right hand traced one of his scars, he flinched.

'I never realised you had so many scars,' she said.

Jeffrey smiled back and pulled her close. 'They're old scars,' he said.

'Well, Luka,' she said, and he smiled at the sound of his new name. 'You

35

won't find any on me.'

'We all have scars,' Luka said. 'It's how you hide them that matters most.'

And the necrosis smiled along with him.

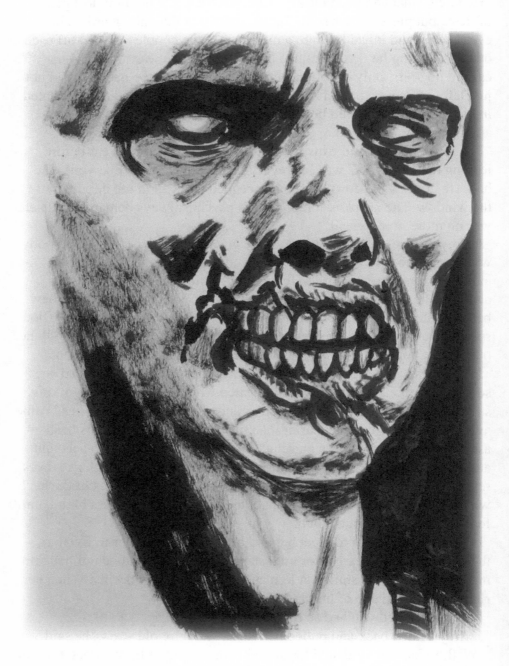

UNREQUITED

"I've met a girl."

Doctor Leanne Munroe gave Donnie a smile. "Really? What's her name?"

Donnie Roberts smiled too and curled his hair nervously. "Sally," he said.

"That's great, Donnie," Dr Munroe said. "I'm really happy for you. It's good that you're moving on."

Donnie kept smiling and scanned the room, staring at the framed medical degrees on the walls decorating Doctor Munroe's psychiatric surgery. It had taken him many months, but he finally seemed comfortable in the surroundings and with Doctor Munroe. He thought of Sally, of how happy he had become, but she still lingered too, deep inside.

"You're still thinking about her aren't you – Monica?"

Donnie's smile faded. Monica suddenly came rushing into his mind; he could see her soft brown hair, smell her fragrance, hear her heart; her heart, beating softly and steadily.

"I know it's hard Donnie," Dr Munroe said. "But you are doing the right thing by moving on. It's been five years since Monica died. Honestly, this is a big step that you're taking here. I'm very proud of you."

Donnie thought of Monica lying still, so still.

"Thanks, doc," he said. "I think Sally's the one you know? She reminds me a lot of Monica."

Donnie could see the psychiatrist was concerned by his last comment. "You can't substitute this girl with Monica, Donnie," she said gently. "It's not healthy. You will only hurt her."

"I know," he said. "It's just that Sally makes me feel alive, like I used to when she was alive."

"That's completely natural, Donnie to feel that way, but you really need to consider why you are with Sally?"

"What do you mean?"

Doctor Munroe put her hand on his. "You can't replace Monica, Donnie. Sally can't be her replacement. Do you understand?"

Donnie turned away and thought of what Sally would look like if she were Monica, if she had brown hair instead of blonde, if she had blue eyes instead of green and if her heart beat like hers.

"Yeah, I understand."

*

The bare skin of Sally's chest was pale and pink, not lightly tanned like Monica's once was. Her breasts were smaller than Monica's too. She even came differently when he was with her. It was quieter. Donnie didn't like it.

"What's the matter?" Sally said breathlessly.

"Why do you do that?" Donnie asked, looking down on her.

"Do what?"

"When you come, you don't make any noise. Why is that?"

Sally frowned and Donnie could see in her eyes that she was about to lie.

"That's just how I come. Why are you asking me about that?" Sally pulled her body away from him, seemingly ashamed. Donnie watched as she abruptly pulled her panties back on and reached for her bra.

"I don't know why I did this," Sally said. "I should never have come here."

Donnie's heart quickened. "You didn't want to have sex with me did you?"

Sally wouldn't look at him.

"She wanted to have sex with me, all the time," Donnie said, forcing Sally to turn.

"Who? Monica?" there was so much disdain in her voice.

"Yes, Monica."

"Well, she's dead Donnie," Sally yelled at him. "She's been dead for a long time. God, what is wrong with you? I thought you wanted to be with me?"

Donnie pulled on his jeans and looked at the floor, Sally's insulting words still stinging his heart. If Monica was alive, her heart would be stinging too...her beautiful heart.

"I thought I did," Donnie said coldly. "But you're nothing like her. You can't ever be like her, not the way you are."

"What the fuck does that mean?" Sally yelled.

Donnie left the room quickly leaving Sally to scream more horrible words. He went to his secret place and found his only memory of his lost love. He wanted to show it to Sally, so she could see what she needed to become if she wanted him to love her. On his way back he grabbed something else from the kitchen.

The scream Sally made when she saw what was in each of his hands, wasn't the reaction Donnie had been hoping for.

*

Doctor Munroe was lead into Donnie Robertson's apartment, up a long dark hallway to a bedroom door. Blood in long spurts covered the walls, the floor, even the ceiling fan. Donnie was seated on the edge of his bed, his whole upper body saturated in the same redness. A blonde girl was lying next to him, a cavernous wound in the middle of her chest.

Formaldehyde was thick in the air, and the source of it was a glass jar that lay in pieces on the floor. Inside the girl's chest was bile yellow-coloured lump of muscle, a long dead heart. Sally own heart was lying in a corner, seemingly tossed away.

Donnie finally spoke, his words choked with tears.

"I thought she would come back," Donnie said. "I thought Sally just needed more heart."

MONGREL

The dog had to die, there were no two ways about it.

Barry had decided that enough was enough; no more barking in the middle of the night, no howling, snarling or scratching. He'd put an end to it once and for all tonight.

He took another swig of his beer and stared over the fence at his neighbour's house. The asshole had only moved in a fortnight ago, but already his dog had pushed Barry to the brink of insanity.

Barry didn't even know the guy had a dog until the first night, when the barking started; Christ he didn't even know the guy's name. All he knew about him was that he had a mangy fucking mutt that was so bored out of its brain it barked and howled each and every night, keeping Barry awake.

The guy must be a shift worker or something, not to have heard his dog carrying on, Barry thought as he took another mouthful. Either that or he was as deaf as a post. Barry finished his beer and turned to gaze at the sunset painted sky; a wash of oranges and pinks. It wasn't something he appreciated anymore, because sunsets always heralded another night of relentless barking.

Barry had complained to the local council and had even sought legal advice. He'd tried to speak to the owner, but he never answered the door and it was hard to tell when he was even at home. Barry had contemplated calling the RSPCA to suggest the dog was being abused or neglected, but he didn't really think it would do any good.

The other neighbours in Barry's street weren't much help either; Dennis Patterson, in number 193, was reluctant to join in on the complaint, despite his well-voiced annoyance. When Barry sought his help, Patterson just nervously cleaned his glasses and went back inside his chamferboard house, pretending as if there was no problem. That was a week ago and Barry hadn't seen or heard from the old buzzard since.

So the only solution left was for Barry to kill the dog.

Funny thing was Barry had never seen the dog. He'd only ever heard it. From the direction of the noise each night, the animal had to be caged up inside the garage. Whatever type of dog it was, it had to be big because its bellows shook the very walls of Barry's house. Then there was the scratching; claws virtually trying to carve a hole in the wall, to be free. Barry was certain the dog would be a danger to everyone in the street if it got out. So in a way, he was doing the neighbourhood a service by killing it.

It wasn't that he hated all dogs, just the ones that had irresponsible owners. Once he shared a flat with a workmate who had a sausage dog; its cuteness only went so far until it started pissing in the clean laundry. What made it worse was the fact his friend found it wholly amusing – even when it pissed on his own clothes.

Barry drained his beer can and walked back into the kitchen, straight for the refrigerator. He glanced at the clock – 6.30 – the barking would commence soon and go on for the rest of the night. He had to act fast. He opened the fridge door and grabbed the plate of raw mince he'd prepared earlier and stared at it.

The plan was simple: wait until nightfall, jump the fence and slip the meat under the back door to the garage. The dog would smell it for sure and bon appétit – one dead dog. Guilt suddenly swarmed in his gut; he thought of the dog eating the mince and slowly succumbing to the poison within; the four or five sprinkles of ant sand Barry had mixed into it. It would surely be a painful death, but didn't the mongrel deserve it?

He'd made up his mind – the barking was going to–

The air seemed to shake as the barking began; a deep resounding rolling voice that Barry imagined was more lion than dog. Then another and another and another in quick succession; each bark resonated in Barry's head and his body couldn't help but flinch in response every time. The bark echoed so loudly Barry swore the canine was standing in his own living room.

Oh, how he hated that dog.

He grabbed a spatula out of the kitchen drawer and scraped the mince into a paper bag. As the cacophony of barking raged on, pounding his ears, Barry slipped the paper bag into his pocket and walked out the back door.

The sun was gone and in its place, high in the sky, sat the moon, like a celestial silver coin. The smell of the jessamine tree flowering in his backyard invaded his nostrils and for a second Barry wondered if it was going to rain. He strolled over to the colour bond fence that separated his property from his neighbour's and stood on his tiptoes to glance over to the other side.

He couldn't see the dog, but he could hear it barking and it was close.

It must have been able to smell him from under the door. As Barry scanned the area he was amazed at how the autumn night seemed to have enveloped everything so quickly and a sense of trepidation set his heart racing. He felt like a kid again, about to pull a prank on one of his mates from school. He only hoped he didn't get caught, because the consequences this time would truly be dire. He turned to look at the back door to the garage and then to the back landing of his neighbour's house. There were no lights on inside, so he felt it was safe to carry on with his plan. With one last check that no one was watching, he pulled himself up and over the fence to the other side.

He landed heavily on his neighbour's lawn, but thankfully the thick grass muffled the sound. As Barry tried to get his bearings, the barking became fiercer. From under the edge of the back door to the garage Barry could hear the dog, snuffling and snarling for him. It so wanted to get out and bite him, but Barry wouldn't give it the chance. Keeping low, he crept up to the door and bent down to peer through the gap.

He jumped when the dog suddenly became crazed with barking, the door shifting as it pushed against it. Then he caught sight of an eye, large and golden yellow. It must be a pit-bull, or a mastiff, Barry wondered. Whatever breed it is it must be something big – too big to be living in the suburbs. Barry doubted if it was even registered.

His mind back on the task, Barry slipped his hand into his pocket and retrieved the meat.

'You want some of this, you little bastard?' Barry whispered to the dog. He heard it whine in response.

'Well, you're gonna love this, buddy boy – you're gonna eat it all up.'

The dog began to scratch on the door and whimper. The fucking thing must be starving, Barry told himself. He tore open the paper bag and began to shove the meat under the door, pushing as much of it through the gap as he could. From the other side he could hear the dog sniffing it.

'That's it – now eat some you fucker!'

The dog sniffed again, but it withdrew, not eager to eat the meat at all.

'What's the matter?' Barry said, perplexed. 'Why aren't you fucking eating the meat?'

The dog growled, low and guttural; its tone had changed. Where the barks had just been noise, or statements of warning before, now when it barked the noises seemed to be made from anger or hatred.

'Just fucking eat the meat!'

The door shook and Barry scrambled backwards in shock. Then the door shook again – so violently that it splintered.

'What the fuck?'

The door exploded, splinters striking Barry in the face. Through the hole came the dog's snavelling head – its massive head. The dog appeared to be way out of proportion, more like a giant Husky or a –

Barry stopped thinking and ran, desperate to reach the fence. Behind him, he heard the door come crashing down and the dog's claws skittering across it. He scrambled for a foothold on the fence, but could not get one. Despite his fear he braved a look at his pursuer and his heart almost stopped.

This was no ordinary dog. It was covered in a thick ash grey coat of fur and its paws were as big as dinner plates. Even though it was hunched down in an attack stance, Barry imagined the dog to be at least five feet high from paw to ear tip and just as long from nose to tail. Then he saw its eyes again, shining wildly in the moonlight. When their eyes met the dog let out a howl, long and low. Barry's blood ran cold.

He tried to scale the fence and failed, falling hard onto his back. Quickly, he turned and tried to stand, but instantly he felt the full force of the animal on his back, like he'd been hit by a truck. The dog wrapped its great jaws around Barry's shoulder and flipped him over like he was a chew toy.

Barry found himself face to face with what could only be described as a hound from Hell.

The dog growled and drool slid from between its fangs – fangs as long and thick as a man's fingers – and splash landed on his Barry's cheek. It was warm and wet and undeniably real. Man and beast, their eyes locked together. Eyes that were so … human.

Barry reached out for something to use as a weapon, his hand searching the lawn. He felt something long and hard and heavy. He gripped it and swung it into the beast's face. It howled in agony and retreated, allowing Barry time to get to his knees.

Bile rose in his throat when he saw his weapon of choice was a bone; too big and long to belong to an animal. His mind screamed at him to throw it away, but it was the only thing he had that gave him any chance of protection from the dog, which was getting ready to pounce again. As he stared in revulsion at the bone, he realised it must have been part of the dog's last meal.

Slowly, Barry stood up and shifted his weight to his feet and he felt something break beneath his shoes. His curiosity was too irresistible and he couldn't help but look down to see what he'd stood on.

A pair of horn-rimmed glasses.

Mr Dennis Patterson's glasses.

Then everything about the bone in Barry's hand made sense and instinctively, he threw it away.

'Oh, fuck!' Barry said more out of horror than realisation.

The dog growled again, but this time the snarl resembled more of a chuckle; in fact Barry was certain the dog was laughing under its breath; laughing at him.

As Barry tried to comprehend the animal, moonlight bled through the clouds, anointing the beast in a viscous white light. Its fur bristled and for a moment, it closed its eyes, like it was savouring the moon's cold embrace. The sight was impossible. The dog was impossible. But then he knew it was much more than just a dog.

The revelation made Barry suck in a breath – a breath that would be his last.

As the dog charged anew, Barry knew the truth:

His neighbour was the mongrel after all.

HARD BARGAIN

The discarded fell relentlessly, like droplets from a tap, from a vein.
Millions of small pieces; bulbous and slick, descending to slap heavily
onto the seething, bleeding, heaving mass below – piled on top of each
other. Some of the discarded would stick, but many would bounce and
tumble off the Mountain, lost to the darkness of the ever-widening crack in
the heavens.

Asmael had no concept of how high Caro Mountain was, but he
understood that it would never cease in its advance. He stared at it in
quiet wonderment; at how it overshadowed him and everything. Over the
millennia the Mountain had outgrown the roof of the neutral territory, with
its steady drip-drip nourishing it and, in turn, the Mountain had developed
a life of its own.

He pulled his tattered shawl around his bone-thin frame and craned his
neck to look at the falling pieces, so high they could have been mistaken
for birds falling to their deaths and not something more precious. He knew
where the pieces fell from; what he could not fathom was why it didn't
stop or what its purpose was.

Asmael almost leapt backwards when a piece unexpectedly landed with
a splash to his right. He'd never seen a piece this close before and an
undeniable twinge of curiosity forced him to drop down and examine it.

It was so red, redder than Asmael's own blood. The moist coating over
it shone with light, which made no sense, because no light could be
harnessed in the neutral territory. Asmael pushed his long hair out of his
eyes and stretched out his hand to touch it; now he knew why he and the
other custodians had to wear the elbow-length leather gloves. The piece
shifted under the pressure of his finger, making a sucking sound as it lifted
off the floor. Asmael had never felt anything so soft, so malleable, so
fragile.

Nervous, he glanced around to make sure no other custodians were
watching. Then he scooped the thing up in his hands.

Juices oozed from it, slipping between his gloved fingers in long amber strings. Disgust rose in his gut as his eyes studied the piece, taking in each bruise, spiralling vessel and pock mark. Whatever it was, it had shape; the inkling of an appendage, perhaps even a tail? To Asmael, it appeared to be the start of something – so why discard it?

Then he felt pressure on his hand, a slight movement. Had the piece moved - of its own accord? Horrified at the thought, Asmael dropped the thing to the ground and the impact sent new waves through it, like shudders or the throes of death. As it struggled to live, it turned itself towards Asmael, reaching for him with its one and only tentacle. The Custodian turned his back on it and closed his eyes tight, desperate to get the vision out of his head.

From the shadows a lone figure began to emerge and Asmael wondered if it was another Custodian – hardly possible when all Custodians had a duty to monitor every slope of the flesh Mountain or risk damnation.

Then the darkness parted and Asmael was astounded to see a human in his midst – dressed in the black garb of an apostle. A priest! Here in the neutral territory? What travesty! Asmael thought. The Custodian watched silently as the priest stopped to take in the sight of the Mountain, seemingly unperturbed by its gruesome majesty.

'Ah, a Custodian,' the priest said.

Asmael didn't know whether to speak as the priest approached him.

'Speak up,' he said. 'What's your name?'

'A – Asmael,' he said, stuttering.

The priest smiled, but it didn't suit him. 'Asmael. Typical.'

Asmael nodded in response, waiting in hope to have permission to speak again.

'What a beauty,' the priest said, beholding the Mountain. Then he considered Asmael again. 'You'd better be taking good care of my asset.'

'Yes, Father, of course,' Asmael replied. Then his curiosity got the better of him. 'Father, please forgive my imposition, but how can you be here, unless you're …'

The priest waved Asmael away. 'That's none of your fucking business is it, peasant? You've got a job to do haven't you? So fuck off and do it!'

Asmael nodded in obedience and attempted to withdraw; to forget the priest and the piece that had twitched in his hand. He turned back to observe the Mountain. Yet the priest remained, standing and watching, as if waiting for something to happen. Asmael bit his tongue, hesitant to even move or breathe.

Still, he needed to know how the priest could be in his midst before the Mountain, uttering such vile language. His mind made up, Asmael defied the twenty-third Commandment and turned to face him.

'Father, forgive me once more, but what are you doing here?'

The priest scowled and dug his teeth into his bottom lip in preparation to spit more foul words, but then the air became enveloped in light and the sound of trumpets. Asmael turned to the impossible light. The Mountain was bathed in it and the Custodian could see the very bottom of the pit that was its throne. The light; the Glory of God was upon them.

'You get back to your fucking post, Custodian!' the priest warned. 'NOW!'

The Custodian turned from the priest and back to the light; it was coming from something; a shape, a man or an –

The angel stepped down from the sky on an invisible staircase, but his flawless feet never touched the ground. Asmael was breaking all the Commandments by looking upon him, but it was not every day a soldier of God entered the neutral territory. The angel turned his head to consider Asmael with eyes made of stars.

'Who is this?' the angel said, each word accompanied by trumpeting.

'Oh, he's just a Custodian – nothing to worry about,' the priest said, an indignant tone in his voice. 'Come on, we need to talk business.'

The angel, his wings concealed under a long golden coat, walked side by side with the priest. 'Will he not hear us?'

The priest looked at Asmael. 'Who gives a shit? As I said, he's just a Custodian.'

'If you have no qualms,' the angel said. 'Then let us discuss the Mountain.'

The Mountain? Asmael thought. Why would they be talking about the mountain?

The priest held out his hand to the Mountain, as if he was trying to capture it all inside his palm.

'Sixty-forty,' the priest said.

The angel looked as if he wanted to scoff, but couldn't.

'I have been sent here to negotiate,' the angel said, straight-faced. 'Not squabble.'

'Aw, come on!' the priest retorted. 'How many clean skins do you get every fucking millisecond of every fucking day?'

The angel never wavered in his steely gaze. 'Yes, yet these "skins" here, as you call them, are untainted.'

The priest kicked the ground, dust spurting into the air. Asmael struggled to comprehend what was happening before him.

'They're trash – fucking pieces of waste that no one wants!'

'Except you,' the angel pointed out.

The priest studied the Mountain again. Asmael could see sweat trickling down his neck.

'Look, okay, okay,' the priest said, his hands out in semi-surrender. 'I'm willing to say fifty-fifty.'

The angel shook his head and somewhere high above, thunder boomed. 'There has to be a balance.'

'How much more balanced can you get than fifty-fifty, for fuck's sake?'

The angel began to walk up the invisible steps. 'If you cannot reach a decision, you will have to wait another one thousand years.'

'No! Wait! Okay – forty-sixty!'

The angel seemed slightly more satisfied. Asmael looked at the Mountain. The Mountain was the currency, something worth bartering over. The seeping, oozing pile of pieces, bulging from the crack in reality was valuable. The thought beggared belief.

'Perhaps that would be worth considering,' the angel said.

'Excuse me?' the priest replied. 'What, do you want more than the majority share? You know that's not how this works. We are allowed to have some of them too.'

The angel puffed out his chest and for a moment the priest looked afraid.

'You stand here in attire that mocks my Father and presume to dictate terms to me? These are souls, just like any other.'

Rage burned [beneath the priest's collar]. 'Souls that have been forsaken,' he said.

'My Father loves each of them.'

'But His precious humanity doesn't – if they did, we wouldn't be here. Don't try and preach to me. Just offer me a reasonable deal.'

The angel contemplated the priest's words and for many minutes Asmael watched him turn over the terms in his mind. Then the glorious creature turned to Asmael and watched him. For a moment the Custodian thought the angel was inside his head.

'You,' the angel said.

'Me?' Asmael replied, terrified.

'What do you say?'

'Him? He's a fucking nobody,' the priest interjected.

The angel turned on the priest, his body flowing with a violent light. 'Be silent!'

'But you can't ask him!'

The angel turned back to the Custodian. 'Will you act as an intermediary?'

48

Asmael quivered and looked to the both of them. 'I don't understand, my lord …'

'You are a Custodian, you watch over these souls every second of every day. You have just as much right to speak on their behalf. If we both offer our reasons, will you decide who receives the greater share?' the angel told him.

Asmael looked to the Mountain and the never-ending supply from above. 'If you tell me what its purpose is – I will decide.'

The angel looked to the priest. 'Do you agree to those terms?'

'Yeah, whatever – just get on with it.'

'Then I will speak first,' the angel said, approaching Asmael. He took the Custodian by the arm and led him to the edge of the great crevasse. They looked upon the Mountain and watched it swell. 'This Mountain is key to God's plan, Asmael,' he explained. 'It offers humanity hope on the eve of its destruction. If you give God the majority of these souls then the balance of good and evil will always turn to the side of good.'

Asmael nodded and watched another piece, another soul, land on top of the pile.

'If you decide to give the majority to him,' the angel said, indicating the priest. 'Then the balance will teeter towards evil and humanity will continue on its path to Armageddon. It is that simple.'

Asmael looked towards the priest. 'Who is he? Is he … the Devil?'

The angel shook his head. 'No, just the executor of his estates, which the Devil only wants to expand.'

Asmael was overwhelmed by the angel's eyes. 'Who are you?'

'Hamerkavah – transporter of God's Glory.'

The Custodian was awe-struck. 'Why should I be given such a task?'

'Because you are free from constraints,' Hamerkavah said. 'You are duty bound to the Mountain and its protection, even if you do not understand it.'

'What is the Mountain?'

'I already told you – it's humanity's salvation.'

Then Hamerkavah walked away to stand back in his place as an observer. The priest quickly appeared by Asmael's side to embrace him like an old acquaintance.

'Hey, Asmael, how you doing, buddy?' the priest said. 'I bet you're in a real kerfuffle – a real tangle of morals. Well, let me tell you right now that that's perfectly normal. We all have to battle with our conscience once in a while, but the beautiful thing about all that misery is that we have a choice. We can decide how we live our lives. You get me?'

Asmael nodded. 'Yes, I think so.'

'So this is why I'm here, why Hamerkavah is here – to make a choice. But, and I'm sure the big guy won't admit to this, he's afraid to make that decision. He's left it up to you, a humble Custodian to make the play.'

'He told me it was because I was duty-bound ...'

'Of course that's what he's going to tell you,' the priest said. 'But he wants you to follow the rules – he doesn't really want you to make a choice.'

The priest looked over the Mountain and smiled. 'You see the mountain, Asmael, well it's the by-product of choice. Shit, the whole human fucking race exists because of choices that were made long ago. God chose to create them and humanity chose to rebel from Him and this Mountain is what God has to live with because of His choices and theirs. You see the picture?'

Asmael swallowed and thought of the Mountain, how he'd watched over it for so long.

'What is it? Hamerkavah never really told me?'

The priest looked back over his shoulder at the angel and shook his head. 'He wouldn't tell you what it is because he doesn't want you to freak out. But, you know what he said about duty? Well, I have a duty to give you all the facts you need to make an informed decision, so I'm going to tell you what it is and why it's so precious. Okay?'

Asmael had waited all his life for this moment; the answer.

'God created Man and woman, right?' the priest said. 'And he told them to go forth and multiply. Well, unfortunately when they ran away from Him, he never got to tell them how to be good parents, how to love them. He never told them that every child is sacred. He never told them not to discard them.'

Asmael felt sick. 'These ... are children?'

'Worse than that – they're aborted children. They're children that nobody wanted. Thrown out like trash. But they're still souls that can be used.'

'What do you want to use them for?'

'We want them to live, that's all. Don't you think they have a right to live?'

'Yes, but what would you do with them?'

The priest smiled. 'You ask a lot of questions, Asmael, but that's good! You want all the information before you make that tough choice. Okay, look. My boss needs people to do certain things in the living world – to keep the balance level. Sometimes those things are bad and when you think about it, these skins or souls are unique enough to perform these tasks. They don't have to be converted or tortured to do our bidding. They're clean and ready to be moulded.'

'So you won't hurt them?' Asmael asked.

'Look, that's not up to me,' he said. 'All I can say is that no one will care if they're hurt. Remember, they've been discarded.'

Asmael saw the Mountain and his heart pained. He'd watched it grow for hundreds of years. It was his life more than anyone else's and just when he was truly beginning to understand it, it was about to be taken away from him. Yet, he was unsure if wanted the responsibility any longer. Suddenly he knew how all the mothers felt; irreversibly torn. He turned to the angel who stood patiently watching the whole affair.

'Must you do this, my Lord?' Asmael asked him.

'Of course he has to – it's part of the arrangement,' the priest said.

The angel came forward. 'The priest is correct. A deal must be reached or all souls will be forfeit.'

'But wouldn't it be better to stop the flow – to end the disposal of souls.'

'Sure it'd be easier,' the priest said, with a snort of derision. 'It'd all be easier if God never created the dumb fuckers in the first place, but hey beggars can't be choosers, right?'

Asmael smiled; for the very first time.

'But I am a beggar and you have asked me to make the choice.'

'But …' the priest complained.

'Let the Custodian make his choice, priest,' the angel warned.

'Fine, let's hear it!'

*

Asmael surveyed the hill that was once a great Mountain breaching the roof of Purgatory.

Since his first smile, when he caught out the demon masquerading as a priest, he hadn't been able to wipe it from his face. Certainly his decision – to split the Mountain in three and give the third portion to an appointed custodian– wasn't his first choice, but it seemed fair from where he was standing.

What he wanted was for the flow of flesh to stop permanently, but the priest had made it clear that the possibility of that occurring was more than rare. The angel meanwhile, had convinced him that God, in all his wisdom, couldn't stop it, even if he wanted to, because it all came down to choice.

Asmael thought back to the first book ever written; how the two central

51

characters, man and woman, had been given a choice and took another path. The Custodian took strength from that choice and made it his own. And his decision was simple: forty percent for the angel; forty for the priest and twenty for him.

The balance would be restored and there would be some left over for Asmael to, what was the word the priest used – love?

Of course, it would only be a matter of time before the hill became a mountain again, but perhaps in another thousand years, humanity would have learned how to staunch the flow themselves?

FEAST OF FEASTS

(FIRST PUBLISHED IN TRICKSTER'S TREATS #3: THE SEVEN DEADLY SINS, 2019 BY THINGS IN THE WELL PUBLICATIONS)

At the trill of the phone, Donald opened his eyes.

Scattered across the bed he called home and atop the rank carpet, were hundreds of bones, new and old, —the relics of his indulgences.

His entire body groaned as he reached for the switch to activate the speaker. For anyone else, the movement would have been almost involuntary, but for Donald— the exertion caused a wave of sweat to break out on his flesh, the liquid mingling with the shit and piss that caked his lower legs. Donald had stopped caring about such things a long time ago.

"Speak," Donald said, his mouth already beginning to water.

Heavy breathing rasped at the other end. "Is this Bruegel? Donald Bruegel?"

Donald shifted, and the bed screamed under his weight. Several bones clattered onto the pile on the floor. Flies buzzed incessantly overhead and crawled across the windows.

"Who is this?"

"Am I talking to Donald Bruegel?"

"Who is this? How did you get this number?" Donald gritted his teeth, the taste of blood setting his heart racing.

"Your aide…what's his name? Marcus? He gave it to me. Or rather, I took it from him."

Panicked, Donald sweated more, perspiration running between the folds beneath his arms, oozing at his crotch.

"Why would Marcus give you this number? Put that fool on the line, now!"

The speaker released a chuckle. "Marcus is dead. I killed him."

"What?" Donald would have sat upright, if it were possible.

"Yeah, I killed him. That's what I do. I've done a lot of killing for you, Mr. Bruegel. You should be more grateful."

Donald swallowed hard as his panic became terror. What would he do without Marcus? For the first time, Donald noticed the room's oppressiveness , its nooks and smells. How would he keep it clean without

Marcus' rare visits? Without Marcus there'd be no one to keep the bed sores under control.. Where would his next meal come from?

"Are you there, Mr Bruegel?" the voice said. Another chuckle. "Of course you are. You've got nowhere to go, have you?"

Donald's stomach demanded to be fed. "Who… are you? What do you want?"

"Well, I know what you want. What you can't do without."

The bed sheets stuck to Donald's skin. He had to do something. Had to get help. But he'd never helped himself before, except to his next meal.

"Didn't you ever wonder where your meals came from?" his tormenter said.

"Marcus… He arranged everything…" Donald said, a sliver of drool escaping his lips.

"Oh, he certainly did. You'd call him, then he'd call me. I'd do my thing and voilà, a delivery would be made right to your filthy front door. Am I right?"

Donald never pondered the 'who' or 'how', all he saw were the cuts of meat, Marcus assured him they were the finest quality.

Now, Marcus was gone forever.

"What is it that you want? More money? I can get you more…"

"See that's the thing, Mr Bruegel. Marcus wasn't doing his job. He'd missed a few payments. I came here to sort things out, but he wasn't very forthcoming so…"

Donald began to blub, tears rolling down his ample cheeks. The saltiness on his tongue set his gut ablaze with desire. "Please…" he said. "I'll give you anything you want."

"What I wanted was never provided. What's needed now is for me to set an example."

"No…" Donald's frame rippled in fear.

"Good luck, you fat fuck!"

The call ended, the engaged signal taunting him on repeat. Donald gazed at his kingdom of waste and his gut roiled. The hunger had to be sated. He swiped his greasy thumb across the phone screen. One of Marcus' associates might be able to help–

The phone slipped from his hand, bouncing off a femur to the floor, beyond reach.

He cried out, his frustration quickly becoming paralysing fear. His heart racing with anxiety, he subconsciously chewed his fingernails. He ran the nails over his tongue for several moments until, desperate for food, he swallowed them down.

Donald Bruegel stared at his fingers for several moments before he decided to have his last meal.

REVANJ

The heady scent of moist soil and blood shook Jerry Thornton back to reality like a slap to the face.

It was impossibly dark and cold and he could feel the touch of midnight dew on his body. In fact, he could feel it all over and as he forced his eyes to pierce the black, he came to the realisation that he was stark naked. His knees rested in the wet grass and his hands were pulled taut away from his sides at right angles.

He was naked, tied up in the dark, in the middle of nowhere and he didn't know why.

The sweat seeping to the surface of Jerry's skin sent a shiver through his spine. His shuddering triggered shards of pain in his jaw and he could taste blood in his mouth. He ran his tongue along his gums and found that at least two teeth were missing. His efforts to work out where he was and how he got there intensified the pain in his head.

He cried out for help as loud as he could, but his echo was the only reply. He pulled at his bonds, but the thick ropes only obliged by cutting deeper into his wrists. His fingers ached in the cold night air and his heart pounded with fear, as if someone was beating on his chest like a drum.

Jerry closed his eyes and tried to breathe, to calm his thoughts. He was smart, he could figure out what had happened. He was always one step ahead. So what went wrong?

He lifted his knees off the ground and crouched into a squat position. The move pulled tighter on his wrists and shoulders, but at least he could take the weight off his knees for a while. He was fairly tolerant of pain, but he couldn't tolerate being taken by surprise.

Slowly Jerry's thoughts came back to him. The last thing he recalled was sitting in Reilly's Bar, enjoying a scotch and the enticing sights around him. He'd been watching a blonde waitress serving drinks; she'd served his scotch and he was enthralled by her casual smile and southern drawl.

He got talking to her and took great pleasure in watching her full lips move with each syllable. He couldn't remember much of what she told him, but he would never forget the angle of her hips and the black silk stockings that seemed to go on forever, all the way up under her ridiculously short skirt. She was lithe and fit, just the way he liked them. He watched her the whole night, enjoying her and his drink. The smoothness of the scotch equalled the smooth look of her fine skin. He planned great plans for her, but then everything went black.

What happened? Jerry shook the beads of cold sweat off his brow and pushed through the pain in his head to think. He'd just been drinking and enjoying the show. How the hell did he end up in this mess and who put him in it? Whoever ruined his plans was going to pay – big time.

His sudden anger flowed into his arms and again he tried to pull himself from his bonds, but all he freed was a scream as his right shoulder threatened to dislocate. The new pain mingled with the one in his jaw and rocked around inside his skull. Nausea quickly followed and before he could stop it, he threw up on the grass. The foul stench of malt whisky and gastric juices burned in his nostrils.

The drink! That was it!

Jerry thought again of the earlier hours of the night. While at the bar he had to use the john and he left his drunk unattended. Some asshole must have spiked my drink and kidnapped me, he realised. Jerry suddenly felt clear and victorious and he shouted out into the night.

"I've figured it out, asshole! You might as well come out!"

There was no reply. No kidnapper. But Jerry wouldn't relent. He knew he had his man.

"Show yourself!"

A sharp scratching sound suddenly struck the air, like steel on stone. There was a tiny spark and Jerry was bathed in a soft golden light. He could see tombstones sprouting out of the grass and a black man sitting in a fold out chair, just metres away, holding a thick, black candle.

He had been sitting there the whole time.

The black man stood and Jerry flinched backwards. His kidnapper must have been more than six feet tall and built like giant. He was dressed in a black wool suit and a floral print silk scarf was tucked tight around his neck. Between his teeth was a cigar.

"Hello, Jerry," he said, with a thick Caribbean accent.

"Who the hell are you?" Jerry yelled back, his scream becoming fog in the freezing air.

"My name is Legrand, Rene Legrand."

"And that's supposed to mean something to me?"

"You don't know me Jerry, but I know you. It has taken me a long time to find you."

Jerry squinted, the light from the candle was actually hurting his eyes. He tried desperately to recognise the black man, this Legrand, but he had never met him in his life. Legrand smiled at Jerry through the cigar smoke.

"What are you smiling at?" Jerry said.

"A man who is helpless for the first time in his life," Legrand said. "The irony is amusing."

"What are you talking about?"

Legrand crouched in front of Jerry and stared at him. Jerry thought there was something not right about the man's eyes.

"I know who you really are Jerry. I know about the secret life that you lead."

Jerry tried hard not to show his surprise. "What do you mean?"

Legrand stood and walked around behind the tombstone. "You like girls."

"What?" Jerry said, exasperated.

"You like watching them. You like seducing them – but not as much as you like raping them and gutting them like fish."

Jerry felt his body trying to pull itself free, the rope stripping the skin off his wrists. His other life was meant to be secret, but somehow this Legrand knew everything about it. The sweat began to pour faster and the drumbeats of his heart pounded deeper and harder.

"What do you want with me?" Jerry heard fear in his voice. He hadn't heard that tone since before his father died.

Legrand gazed into the candle. He wouldn't look at Jerry. The flame seemed to jerk towards Legrand's lips as he spoke. "There was a girl – here in Memphis. You watched her. You seduced her. Then you raped and gutted her. Do you remember?"

Jerry tried to focus on getting free, but he could not look away from the flame reflected in Legrand's murderous eyes.

"Do you remember her?!" Legrand's breath shook the flame.

Jerry recalled the last girl in Memphis. It was about a year ago in yet another bar with yet another girl – a black girl. She was sexy, with skin like melted chocolate. He conquered her and left her to die in the swampy marshlands of the Deep South.

"You knew her?" Jerry muttered.

Legrand slammed his hand down on the tombstone and Jerry thought it would break. "She was my kin!"

Jerry's head dropped, but oddly he didn't feel afraid, he felt like laughing – and that's exactly what he did.

"You're family," Jerry's whole body rocked with laughter. "That's just perfect!"

"Do not laugh at me!"

Legrand's bellow shook Jerry's bones and he stopped laughing. The huge black man strode over and gripped Jerry's tiny jaw in his hand and squeezed. Jerry wailed as he felt bone crunch on bone. Legrand's eyes were as black as the night that swarmed around them.

"You will not laugh again – not after this night!" Legrand told him.

Legrand slapped Jerry across the face. Then he left him, striding back to his place behind the tombstone. He picked up the candle and poured hot wax over the stone. The drops looked like foul blood. Then the Negro started to whisper and chant and move, as if he was caught in some strange waltz of madness.

"What are you going to do?" Jerry begged him.

Legrand kept on with his barbaric dance, leaping and twirling through the candle smoke. Jerry watched as Legrand retrieved a small cloth bag from his coat. In a seamless rhythm, the big man emptied its contents onto the wax. The dust lingered in the air like flakes of ash.

"Let me go!" Jerry pleaded.

Legrand ignored him and instead tore off his coat and shirt, revealing a muscled torso, slick with sweat. His eyes were glazed white and Jerry wondered if he could even hear him anymore. Jerry's fear swelled and he tried again to free his hands. Legrand pounded on the top of the tombstone, boom-boom-boom, boom-boom-boom, over and over, a crescendo that quickened the pace of Jerry's already screaming heart. Jerry pulled and pulled at his bonds until finally his shoulder popped in wrenching agony. His scream became the climax of Legrand's sickening ballet.

"This pain you feel now," Legrand said, suddenly beside Jerry again. "Is nothing compared to what she felt. You cut her and stabbed her and bled her dry into the ground Jerry, but so much more will you feel."

Legrand painted Jerry's face with the wax-tainted ash and sneered.

"She will relish this."

"Who is she?" Jerry screamed through the pain.

Legrand leaned back, and like a crazed game show host, he underlined the name on the tombstone with his hand, a great toothy grin on his face. The engraved letters shimmered in the candlelight and Jerry feared the name had come to life:

Marie Legrand.

Legrand stood over Jerry and smiled. "She was my daughter and you killed her. It took me a long time to find you Jerry, but eventually all your girls led me to you. Their bodies spoke to me and told me where you would be – tis strange that you would come back to the same town where you first met my Marie."

"Look, I'm sure that nothing I say will go as an apology, but I think we can both safely say that I have a problem," Jerry explained. "I need help. But I'm also very wealthy. I could repay you for your loss."

Now Legrand laughed – a laugh that seemed to come from the depths of hell.

"Repay me? You do not need to repay me, Jerry Thornton."

The air was still, but the ground beneath Jerry's knees began to shake and split. The grass at the base of Marie Legrand's tombstone burst upwards and maggots, in the hundreds began to crawl to the surface. Jerry tried to scream, but no sound would come. He could only gape at the squirming, slithering mass as it swelled higher and closer.

Yet something else stirred under the moving carpet of living filth – something much larger. How slowly it emerged; five mottled stalks broke through and wriggled more freely than the worms. At first, Jerry thought they were stems, but then he saw the fingernails at the tips.

The rotten hand pushed the worms aside with ease and stretched out of the ground. Jerry jerked and pulled at the rope around his right wrist and surprisingly he slipped free. When he forced himself to turn away from the thing coming out of the ground to look at the rope, he beheld the skin of his right hand hanging between the bonds. He shrieked in agony.

But Jerry's cry was cut short. Feeling the cold, dead hand on his shoulder, he turned back to see more of its owner bearing down on him. The corpse was half-free from its grave; its skull was almost stripped bare of flesh, its teeth cracked and brittle in its jaw. Spiralling threads of raven black hair were scattered about its crown, but its abyss-like eye sockets were what burned Jerry's heart the most.

He swatted its hand away, but it just kept reaching for him and crawling towards him. Jerry tried to free his left hand, but his raw right hand was a useless mass of blood – blood that he knew the corpse could smell.

"Look at my Marie," Legrand cried. "Isn't she beautiful?"

Marie's corpse pulled itself along the ground towards Jerry, as if he was its one singular purpose in death. It shuffled on its ribcage towards him, making a squelching sound on the bloody carpet of maggots. Its hips broke free of the ground, then its thighs and finally its feet.

Jerry began to scrape and pick at the broken flesh of his left wrist like a man possessed. He didn't want to look at Marie's corpse. It wasn't real. She was dead and he killed her. One year ago. He raped her and then he slit her from crotch to throat. He watched her bleed out into the swampy waters of the Mississippi. He left her for dead.

He felt tears on his face as Marie's corpse reached for him; its clawlike fingers digging deep into the flesh of his thigh. He kicked it away, but it just kept coming. He felt its fingers again, this time groping at his stomach. He tried to fight it off, but he knew it would never stop.

Jerry bellowed and writhed, but Legrand's laughter was even louder than his screams. Marie's corpse bit into his chest and neck and Jerry felt his blood explode into the air. The last thing he saw was Marie Legrand's blood-soaked teeth sink into his eye.

The last thing he heard was Rene Legrand's voice:

"Don't worry Jerry, I not finished wit' you yet."

THE FAMILY BUSINESS

My Daddy had a very special job.

Every day, he packed his special bag with his special tools and he trudged off down the road, whistling his favourite tune.

My Daddy never worked in an office like most people, no the streets were his office and he wouldn't have it any other way.

"The world is your oyster," he used to tell me.

I'll never forget the first time he took me to his work. I was so excited. We walked hand in hand along Manson Street and I listened to him whistling Dixie. He's so strong and tall, but I didn't mind having to look up at him. He was like my own personal Goliath.

On that day we stopped at number 42 Manson Street and went through the gate; the squeak of its rusty hinges sounded almost like Daddy's special tune.

He looked at me and smiled: "Now we knock on the door and wait."

After a few minutes the door opened and a short, plump woman greeted us with a smile. Daddy shook her hand and started his speech:

"Good Morning Mrs Robertson," he said. "I'm from the Repossession Agency. I've come to talk to you about your inappropriate use of our products."

"Excuse me?" the lady said, looking confused.

She looked to me, but I just kept smiling, like Daddy always told me to do.

"Might we talk about it inside?" Daddy asked.

The lady nodded and stepped aside to let us in and I noticed her forehead was all sweaty-looking.

Daddy strode into the living room, which was filled with bright orange lounge chairs and decorated with daffodil print wallpaper. I thought the whole room looked ugly. Daddy placed his special bag on the dinner table. Next to it was an ashtray, with a lighted cigarette twirling smelly smoke into the air.

"What's this all about, Mr …?"

"Agent Samson, ma'am," Daddy corrected her. "This is about your recent appropriation of organs supplied by our company."

"Beg yours?" Mrs Robertson said.

"Your kidneys."

I watched Mrs Robertson slide her hands to her back. She looked from me to my Daddy. The sweat was running down her face.

"We've been made aware that you haven't been following our doctor's instructions. That you've been abusing our gift."

The company Daddy worked for keeps people alive. They sell organs, livers, kidneys, hearts, but watch out if you don't look after them.

"You've started drinking alcohol again haven't you, Mrs Robertson?"

The lady shook her head, but even I knew she was lying.

Daddy walked into the lady's kitchen and opened the fridge. There were beer bottles inside. Daddy frowned upon alcoholics; he said they were "weak and lazy in life".

"You can't take my kidneys!" Mrs Robertson suddenly screamed. I jumped with fright, but Daddy always protected me.

Mrs Robertson ran from the living room up the hall, but Daddy was on her tail. He yelled at me to bring his bag, but I could hardly hear him over Mrs. Robertson's screams.

When I got to Mrs. Robertson's bedroom I handed Daddy his bag and he took it with his left hand because his right was wrapped around the lady's throat. She was thrashing like a caught fish, but Daddy's grip was very strong. He put the bag aside and then slapped her hard across the face. She went to sleep straight away.

"You stay there now, son," Daddy told me.

I backed into the corner, near the bedroom door and stood like a statue and went as quiet as a mouse. I watched Daddy very carefully. He shifted Mrs Robertson up the bed and took off her pink nightgown, to reveal a skin-tight nightie. Mrs Robertson was a big lady and her nightie was so tight it looked like the wrapping around cookie dough.

Daddy unzipped his special bag and pulled out a pair of shears. He snipped the nightie open from top to bottom and Mrs Robertson's bosoms flopped out as if they were grateful to be free. I'd never seen another woman's bosoms before, except Mommy's. Hers are much nicer than Mrs Robertson's.

I stared as Daddy reached under her back and flipped her over onto her stomach. She was very much asleep and heavy looking. Daddy put the shears back in his bag and then he pulled out a long, sharp knife.

This was always my favourite part.

63

I got to see why Daddy was paid the big bucks.

Underneath the skin of Mrs Robertson's back was a big gloppy mess that reminded me of creamed corn. Beneath that was bright red, meaty muscle. Daddy sliced through it easily with the knife and I could see a deep, dark hole.

"Come have a look son," Daddy said.

I walked over and looked inside the blackness of the hole before Daddy plunged his bare hand inside.

"The people I work for are very generous people," Daddy explained as he felt around inside Mrs. Robertson. "They grow organs to keep people alive, but unfortunately, some of the people they give these organs to don't appreciate what they've been given and they waste them. Just like Mrs. Robertson here."

He pulled out a baked bean-shaped lump of slimy, greenish coloured meat.

"Mrs Robertson was given two new kidneys, to keep her alive and she has abused them. See?"

He showed me the bruises on the surface and I nodded to show I understood.

"When did your bosses first start making organs, Daddy?" I asked as he began to cut into the right side of the lady's back.

"January 2, 2020 - the day after New Year; they came on the television and told us about how doctors had finally figured out how to grow organs from people's own tissue. There would be no more need for organ donors. No more anti-rejection drugs.

"But with the news came a strict set of rules that have to be followed. The Repossession Agency was formed to uphold those rules."

Daddy removed the other kidney and slipped them both inside a clean bag. Then he placed the bag carefully inside the special bag.

"That was before I was born wasn't it, Daddy?"

"Yes son."

"What will happen to those kidneys, Daddy?" I asked.

"Unfortunately, we can't give them to anyone else son, but we'll keep them, for posterity. Do you know what that word means?"

I thought hard. "Um, when you can remember something?"

Daddy chuckled. "That's pretty close. It's so that future generations – your children and your children's children will remember why we did what we did."

"Oh," I said.

Daddy packed up his bag and led me out the bedroom door. I had one last glance over my shoulder at Mrs. Robertson's bloody body as we walked up the hall. We left the house with the ugly orange furniture behind and as we started to walk back along Manson Street towards home, I could tell by Daddy's whistle that his work was done.

*

Looking back on that day, I think Daddy's words about 'posterity' aren't quite correct. We didn't exactly keep Mrs Robertson's kidneys. We never actually keep any of the organs that Daddy repossesses, well, not in a physical sense at least. They don't hang on the mantelpiece.

This is where Mommy comes in. She works for the company too, helping Daddy keep the organs that people never really wanted. It was many years before I figured out how Mommy helped Daddy, but she wasn't just helping him, she was helping all of us.

That night, after going with Daddy to his work for the first time, we all remembered what Mrs Robertson wasted. All of us, Mommy, Daddy and my brother Bobby and sister Alice, all sat around the dinner table and remembered. Daddy said Grace and then we ate - steak and kidney pie.

It was a beautiful way to remember how important Daddy's job is.

We all have a job in the company now. Daddy was a Repossessor and he trained me to be a Repossessor. Bobby will one day become a Repossessor and Alice will help Mommy keep the organs for posterity.

*

Although Daddy trained me on all the ways to be a good Repossessor, the company has to approve all Agents.

When I wanted to become an Agent, I had to go to the 'Factory', the place where they made the organs that saved people's lives. Daddy and I dressed in dark suits and we drove into the city. The Company's headquarters was the biggest and shiniest building in the city, like Heaven on Earth.

I met the Director, Mr Bundy. He was much older than Daddy and a lot skinnier and he seemed like a really smart man. He took me to the testing room, where all the Agents go for their examination. But first, there was the interview. Mr Bundy sat me down in a chair inside a white room. Four other people entered and sat down with Mr Bundy to stare at me.

"So you want to follow in your father's footsteps?" Mr Bundy asked.

"Yes. I want to be a Repossessor."

65

"Do you know what the position entails?" Mr Jones said.

"My father has taught me all there is to know about being an Agent. He is a great teacher."

"Indeed," Mr Bundy said. "He has served us well."

"Until recently,' Mr Jones interjected.'

This was puzzling. It appeared Daddy had done something wrong that had offended Mr Bundy and the other Directors.

"Is there something wrong?" I said.

Mr Bundy shared a look with Mr Jones and then sighed at me.

"Your father has neglected his gift. He has squandered it."

His gift? What gift could he have? I thought. He had been an agent for the Company for years ensuring only good people received what they deserved.

"I'm sorry," I said. "But what do you mean?"

Mr Jones's eyes were dark and digging into me.

"His heart. He has misused it."

That didn't make sense. Daddy's heart was just fine. He's never had any problems with it as far as I knew. Then it dawned on me. I'd only known my father since I was born, eighteen years before. I had no idea of the life he led before then.

I thought he was meant to tell me everything?

I looked at Mr Bundy and Mr Jones directly.

"What do you need me to do?"

*

I'll never forget the first time I took my brother Bobby with me on my first job. I was a newly initiated agent and my brother was eager to learn.

The job was at number 22 Crowley Street – our family home. I walked hand in hand with Bobby up to the front door. I knocked and waited for someone to answer the door.

Daddy answered and he had such pride in his eyes for me.

"Mr Samson?" I asked.

"Yes?"

"I'm an Agent from the Repossession Agency. I'm here to discuss your … inappropriate use of our gift."

Daddy suddenly looked shocked. He clutched his chest.

"My heart?"

"Yes, sir," I replied. "You … have misused it. For your own gain. You have sinned two-fold. Repossessor's are not meant to love. Organs are not meant to be squandered."

Daddy didn't struggle. He just let me in. He led me outside, to the garage.

"I don't want it done in my home," Daddy told me.

"I understand, sir."

Daddy smiled at me and studied my appearance.

"You look like an Agent should, son."

"Thank you sir, I learned from the best."

The statement brought a tear to his eye, but he wiped it away and opened the garage door. We stepped inside and he closed it again. For a moment we were in darkness, but then Daddy clicked on the overhead light. I saw him standing there with his shirt open, a long vertical scar on his chest.

"Make it quick son."

"Yes sir."

I hit Daddy hard on the jaw and he fell like a stone. He was sleeping soundly, without fear. I pulled off his shirt and ran my finger over the old scar. I turned to Bobby and encouraged him inside.

"An Agent once told me that the Company is like God. They bestow gifts upon people and if they follow the laws set down by the Company, then they get to live."

"Did Daddy break the rules?" Bobby asked.

I turned to Daddy and slipped the knife in his chest, just at the tip of the sternum. It disappeared under the ribcage and from there I cut a window for Bobby to see Daddy's beating heart.

"This man became an Agent at eighteen. At 25, his heart failed, but the Company gave him a new one. Having pledged himself again to the Company, he set back to his job as a Repossessor. On his thirtieth birthday, he met a woman, who would become our Mommy. He fell in love with her, which under the Act is a misappropriation of gifts given."

I reached into Daddy's chest and with the knife separated his heart from the aorta. My suit was soaked with Daddy's blood. Bobby was pale, but I held his hand.

"But before Daddy died he passed on the rules to me and Mommy and you and Alice, so we would never forget. It's all about 'posterity' Bobby."

Bobby nodded in understanding.

We left the garage and went to seek Mommy's help.

*

That night we gathered at the table to remember Daddy and keep him sacred.

Mommy prepared a beautiful meal in his honour. His words, his rules, his beliefs will be with us always. I'll never forget the taste of everything he ever stood for.

He may have broken the rules, but at least he died by them.

Thank you, Daddy.

Two-time international Bram Stoker Award-nominee®* and multiple Australian Shadows Award nominee, Greg Chapman is a horror author and artist based in Queensland, Australia.

Greg is the author of several novels, novellas and short stories, including his award-nominated debut novel, *Hollow House* (Omnium Gatherum) and collections, *Vaudeville and Other Nightmares* (Specul8 Publishing) and *This Sublime Darkness and Other Dark Stories* (Things in the Well Publications).

He is also a horror artist and his first graphic novel *Witch Hunts: A Graphic History of the Burning Times*, (McFarland & Company) written by authors Rocky Wood and Lisa Morton, won the Superior Achievement in a Graphic Novel category at the Bram Stoker Awards® in 2013.

He was also the President of the Australasian Horror Writers Association from 2017-2020.

* Superior Achievement in a First Novel for Hollow House (2016) and
Superior Achievement in Short Fiction, for "The Book of Last Words" (2019)

Made in United States
Troutdale, OR
10/09/2023

13545139R00043